Grandma and her Chocolate Labrador

Traitor Dachshund, the children's imprint of Minted Prose, LLC
New York

www.traitordachshund.com

Grandma and her Chocolate Labrador is a work of fiction. Names, characters, places, and events were created by the author. Any resemblance to actual events, places, or persons, living or dead, is purely coincidental.

Library of Congress Control Number: 2014933003

ISBN 978-0-9905721-8-3

Printed in USA

Grandma and her Chocolate Labrador

By P. J. Fischer

Illustrations by Cindy Nguyen

TRAITOR DACHSHUND
NEW YORK

Grandma waved goodbye as her family moved away.

“Don’t forget to write,” Grandma called.

CALIFORNIA

"It feels so quiet,"
Grandma thought.

Grandma opened a big photo album on her lap.
She looked at the picture of her old room.

"I was so happy as a child," she sighed.

Grandma hadn't been in the attic for years.

There she found some old friends.

She played

and played

and then saw her fish bowl.

So she went to the store
to find a fish.

Mr. Fish swam back and forth.
Grandma felt a little better.

She decided to play in
the dining room!
She laughed and laughed.

shopping list:
milk
eggs
bread

But something was missing,
so Grandma decided to
host a tea party.

Something was still missing.

"I remember something else that made me happy. I loved planting trees,"

Grandma thought.

"Planting trees!"

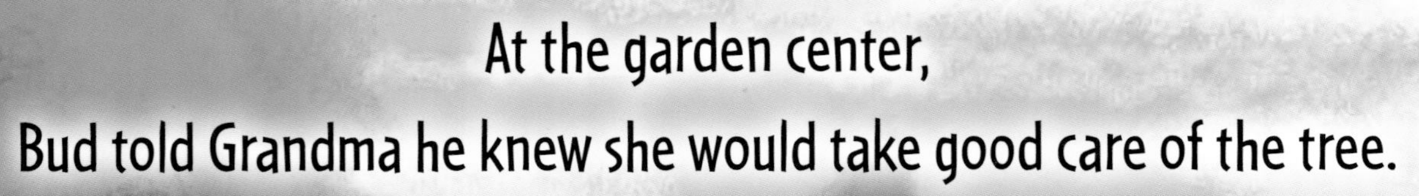

At the garden center,
Bud told Grandma he knew she would take good care of the tree.

"A little water and sunshine is all anybody really needs," Bud said.

Grandma took the tree home and planted it.

Still Grandma knew
something was missing.

"I just miss my old dog Buddy,"
Grandma told herself.
"But I don't know if I can take care of a dog at my age."

Grandma went to the shelter.

All the puppies were already adopted, so she got the next best thing.

Mr. Goat didn't play well
at the doggie playground.

But some time later the neighbor boy had a surprise.

"Our dog had puppies," he said.

Grandma adopted the puppy
and named him Chocolate.
As time passed,
Chocolate settled in at
Grandma's house.

Grandma had a new friend at last.
They played and played. . . . And she laughed and laughed.

"Go get it, Chocolate!"
Grandma called.

"All anyone needs is a little water, a sunny day, and some good friends to share it with!" Grandma said.

The kids used to be so small,
but they were growing up.
Just like Chocolate.

Chocolate had grown to be
Grandma's best friend.

P. J. Fischer was the little kid who lived around the corner from his grandmother. He used to bike over and stay a while! Back then, the author's dog was named Mustard.

"My family was one big smash up of eight kids, parents, grandparents, relatives, dogs, chickens, and rabbits," Fischer said. "Everyone was in the mix and Grandma was always there."

Remembering those sweet times, Fischer created *Grandma and her Chocolate Labrador*. In *Grandma and her Chocolate Labrador*, Grandma's inner life is shared with readers. This book is a starting point for discussing the importance of friendship at any age. It is a spirited call to action for a family to prevent older members from feeling lonely. It also shows the role that a pet can play as a friend and companion. In our story, Grandma takes charge and in the process true love springs forth. We hope you enjoy this wonderful tale!

Cindy Nguyen of Gau Family Studio, Des Moines, Iowa, is the lead illustrator for *Grandma and her Chocolate Labrador*. Gau Family Studio worked closely with Traitor Dachshund to create beautiful custom illustrations for this story.